This edition published by Parragon Books Ltd in 2015 and distributed by

Parragon Inc.
440 Park Avenue South, 13th Floor
New York, NY 10016
www.parragon.com

Written by Diane Muldrow
Illustrated by Scott Tilley and Brent Ford

ISBN 978-1-4723-9640-2

Printed in China

Mickey's Spooky Night

PaRRagon

Bath · New York · Cologne · Melbourne · Delhi
Hong Kong · Shenzhen · Singapore · Amsterdam

Mickey Mouse looked around his living room with pride.
It was decorated with ghosts, spiders, and bats.
A jack-o'-lantern smiled at him from the mantelpiece.
   "I'm going to have the greatest Halloween party tonight,"
Mickey said to himself as he tacked one last fake cobweb
to the wall. "Now, it's time to make some snacks!"

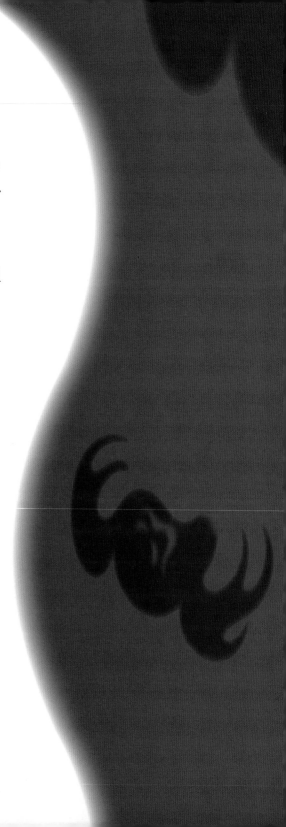

Mickey went to the kitchen
and began making popcorn.
Suddenly, he noticed something
moving around in the backyard.
He picked up a candle, opened
the door, and peeked outside.

The moon was full and it was
very windy, so the branches and
leaves on the trees were making
lots of strange shadows.

"Gosh," said Mickey, shaking
his head as he went back
inside. "I'm just being silly!"

Mickey glanced at the clock. "Oh dear, it's almost time for the party—and I still have to get ready!" he exclaimed. "Now, where did I put that old pirate costume?"

Mickey went upstairs and climbed up, up, up a ladder into the dark attic. As soon as he switched on the light . . . *CRASH!* Thunder boomed and lightning flashed across the sky, making Mickey jump.

As Mickey looked around the attic, he noticed something tall and dark in the corner. He crept closer, holding his breath. Then a huge, ghostly shadow fell over him.

"Uh, h-h-hello?" Mickey whispered nervously.

BOOM! Thunder rumbled and lightning flashed again, revealing the eerie figure Mickey had been scared of. It was just a coat rack with a sheet over it!

"Oh, silly me," Mickey chuckled to himself. "Scared of an old coat rack!"

In the corner of the attic, Mickey found an old trunk covered in cobwebs and dust. "I'll bet my pirate costume is in here!"

He brushed the dust off the top, turned the key in the rusty lock, and slowly opened the lid. . . .

"Aagghh!" Mickey screamed. A skeleton popped right out of the trunk!

Mickey jumped back in horror before he realized it was just a plastic party decoration

"Phew—I guess the joke's on me!" Mickey sighed as he rummaged through the trunk.

Underneath his pirate costume, Mickey found lots more Halloween decorations.

"These would be great for the party!" he said excitedly. "I'd better take the whole trunk downstairs. The gang is going to love all these decorations!"

Meanwhile, Pluto was chasing a ball around Mickey's backyard. As he charged under the clothesline, a big, white sheet came loose from the line and fell on him. He was covered from head to tail!

Suddenly, it began to rain, making the
sheet wet so it stuck to Pluto like glue! He
ran all over the yard, but—no matter how
hard he tried—he couldn't shake it off!

Minnie, Donald, Daisy, and Goofy arrived at Mickey's house. "Mickey!" they called. "We're here!"

But Mickey couldn't hear them over the sounds of the storm. Suddenly, the lights went out! Then, they heard strange dragging sounds coming from upstairs.

Minnie gasped. "What was that?"

With the storm, the dark, and the creepy noises—it felt like they were in a haunted house!

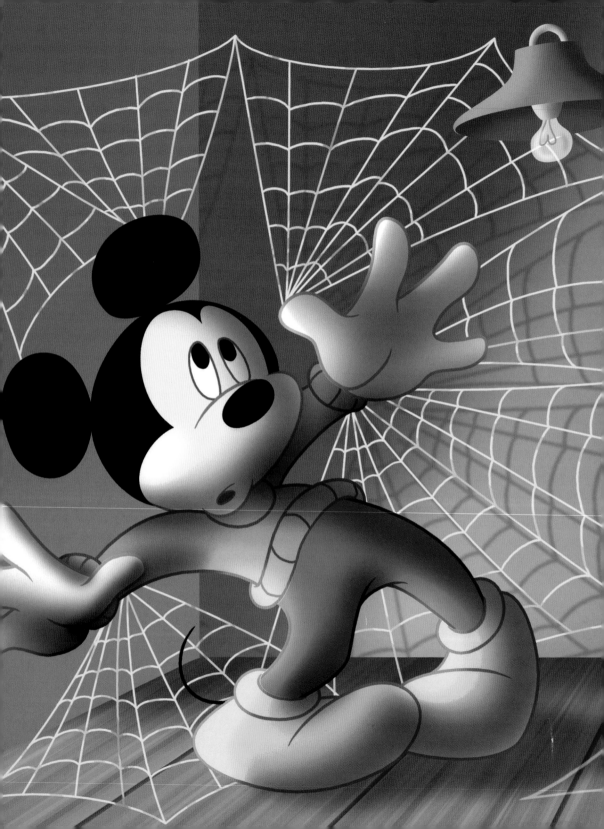

Up in the attic, Mickey stopped dragging the trunk. He decided it was too heavy to take all the way downstairs. As he searched for a flashlight, he walked straight into a huge cobweb!

"Yikes!" Mickey cried. "These cobwebs are all over the place!"

Finally, he found a candle and some matches.

"The gang will be here soon," Mickey thought. "I'd better change into my costume!"

Meanwhile, poor Pluto was still trapped under the sheet! He raced around the backyard, trying to find his doggy door.

Daisy heard strange noises coming from outside. "What's that sound?" she asked.

Daisy and Goofy peeked out the window and saw an eerie white shape running past. Daisy gasped.

"It's a g-g-ghost!" cried Goofy.

The two friends screamed and quickly shut the window. This Halloween party was getting scarier by the minute!

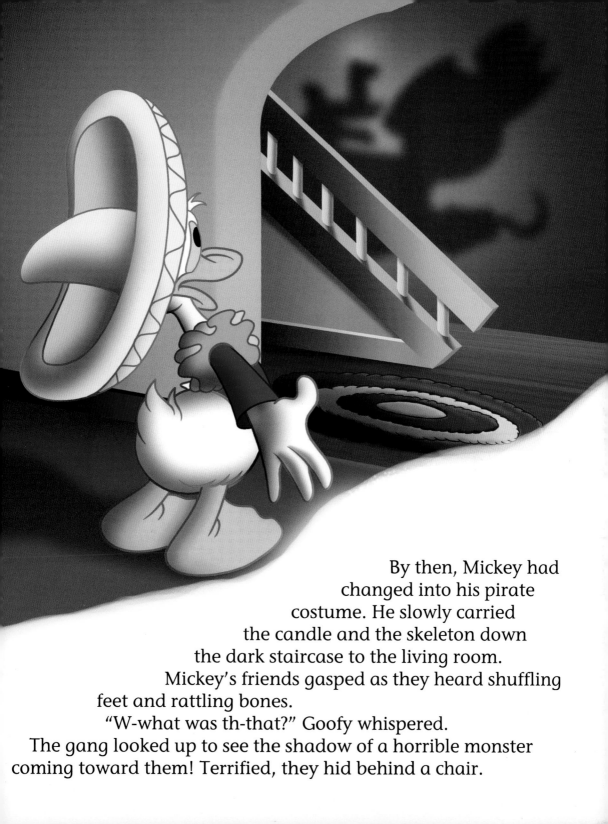

By then, Mickey had
changed into his pirate
costume. He slowly carried
the candle and the skeleton down
the dark staircase to the living room.
Mickey's friends gasped as they heard shuffling
feet and rattling bones.
"W-what was th-that?" Goofy whispered.
The gang looked up to see the shadow of a horrible monster
coming toward them! Terrified, they hid behind a chair.

Just then, the lights came back on.
"Gosh! Hiya, gang!" Mickey cried,
surprised to find his friends cowering behind
a chair.
"Oh, Mickey!" Minnie sighed. "It's just you!
You really scared us."

"We thought you were a ghost!" cried Goofy.
"That's one scary costume!" Daisy added,
pointing to the hook on Mickey's hand.
"Sorry, guys," Mickey apologized. "Now,
let's get the party started!"

Just then, Pluto found his way in through
the doggy door. Still covered in the white sheet,
he ran into the living room.

"It's the g-g-ghost!" cried Minnie.

The friends jumped and screamed as Pluto
ran around frantically, bumping into Mickey.

Suddenly, Mickey noticed the ghost had a tail.

"Wait a minute . . . ," he said, grabbing the sheet and revealing Pluto. "Oh, Pluto! It's just you!"

Mickey hugged Pluto and dried him with a towel. He smiled at his friends.

"You know, with all these ghosts, shadows, and noises—this is the scariest Halloween ever!"